Starship Football

David Orme

Illustrated by Paul Savage

Titles in Full Flight

Abducted by an Alien	Jonny Zucker
Summer Trouble	Jonny Zucker
Sleepwalker	Jillian Powell
The Reactor	Jillian Powell
Starship Football	David Orme
Race of a Lifetime	Tony Norman
Speedway	Tony Norman
Goalkeepers	Jonny Zucker
Your Passing Was Rubbish and other poems	ed. Jonny Zucker
Real Radio - a play	Jonny Zucker

Badger Publishing Limited
26 Wedgwood Way, Pin Green Industrial Estate, Stevenage,
Hertfordshire SG1 4QF
Telephone: 01438 356907. Fax: 01438 747015.
www.badger-publishing.co.uk   enquiries@badger-publishing.co.uk

Starship Football   ISBN 1 85880 925 8

Series Editor: Jonny Zucker.
Publisher: David Jamieson.
Editor: Paul Martin.
Cover design: Jain Birchenough.
Cover illustration: Paul Savage.

Starship Football

David Orme

Illustrated by Paul Savage

Contents

Badger Publishing

Chapter 1 - Todd's Problem

Todd knew that he was lucky. Most boys of his age never went into space.

But Todd's mum and dad were part of the crew of a huge starship. The ship, called The Searcher, went on missions across the galaxy.

There were nearly two thousand people on the ship. The crew could take their families with them.

There was always plenty to do on the ship. But Todd and his friends had a problem. They lived for the one thing they couldn't do on the starship.

They loved football.

Of course, they could watch as much
football as they liked. All the big
matches between planets were shown
on the starship TV.

They could even play 'virtual' football.

You put on a helmet and a special suit, and stood on a platform. As you moved about the floor moved under you! You felt as if you were running about and kicking, just like in a real game. But you didn't really move very far at all.

Todd's gang wanted to play real football, but there wasn't anywhere to play.

"You can't play real soccer on a starship," Todd's Dad explained. "There's no room for a pitch."

Chapter 2 - The All-Stars

Todd and his football mad friends had made up a fantasy five-a-side team called 'Searcher's All-Stars'.

- Todd was striker.
- Mick and Tony played mid-field.
- Tim was big and beefy, so he was in defence.
- Becky was goalie.

One day after school they were sitting in the rest room. Captain Robins came in. Todd's friends were surprised.

The captain didn't often come into the rest room. He was much too important!

Becky knew the captain well. Her
mother worked on the ship's bridge.
The captain waved to her.

"Hello gang," he said. "Finished school
for the day?"

Todd thought quickly. Maybe they
could get the captain on their side!

"Excuse me, Captain Robins," he said. "We're the Searcher's All-Stars. We're mad about football, but there's nowhere to play. Can you help?"

Captain Robins smiled. "I'm a football fan myself! I support Manchester Galactic!"

"But there's not much room on a starship, you know."

Todd groaned to himself. That was what Dad had said!

The captain went on. "And even if there was, one team's no good. You need someone to play!"

Chapter 3 - The Challenge

The captain was right. You need two teams for a football match!

The captain had made a note of Todd's name. He said he would see what he could do, but what could he do when there was only one team and no room?

Todd was amazed when a message came from the captain three days later. He showed it to his parents.

CHALLENGE!

The Searcher's All-Stars are
challenged to a special

FIVE-A-SIDE
FOOTBALL
MATCH

In hold 5c
In seven days time.

Signed

Captain Robins

Manager, Searcher's United.

Dad laughed. "Good old Captain
Robins! Hold 5c is empty on this trip.
It's a big space - just right for football!"

"But who are Searcher's United?"
Dad didn't know, but Becky did. She
had heard about it from her Mum.

"The captain's really keen. Some of the crew have played real football before. They've made up a team to play us!"

Playing the crew! Todd wasn't sure. Some of the spacemen on the ship were very tough.

"What do we do?"

"Accept the challenge!" said Tim. "We can't back out now!"

Todd wrote accepting the challenge. The captain wrote back telling him that they could use hold 5c for team practice. He said that he would referee the game. He promised to be fair!

Chapter 4 - Practice

The crew had worked hard to turn the
big empty hold into a football pitch.
Lines were painted on the floor, and
goals had been set up. Straight after
school, the All-Stars had their first
practice.

There were soon problems. Todd knew all about football, and the five-aside rules. But this wasn't the same as really playing. He got the team to practice skills such as dribbling, passing the ball, and tackling, but they needed real match practice.

Everyone agreed that Becky was their best player. She didn't need to learn how to keep goal - she was a natural player. Time and again Todd fired the ball at the goal, but not much got past her.

The All-Stars might not score many goals - but with Becky in goal, maybe the crew wouldn't either!

The final practice session had just finished. The match was tomorrow.

"One good thing," said Tony. "The hold is only big enough for the players. No-one else will see how badly we do."

As they were leaving the hold, they met two crew members coming in.

"What's going on?" asked Mick.

"We're setting up cameras. Didn't you know? Everyone's got so interested in the game that it's going out live. The whole ship will be watching!"

Chapter 5 - The Big Match

The captain had set the game up really well. Special football strips had been made.

- The All-Stars wore blue, with white stars.
- United were in red, with a picture of the Searcher across their chests.

The crew team looked very big. Todd felt his knees shaking. He hoped it didn't show on TV!

Captain Robins was wearing referee's clothes. He asked Todd to shake hands with the captain of the crew's team.

This was Charlie Burnet, who worked with Todd's Dad. Charlie was really friendly. Todd felt better straight away.

Todd kicked off, passing the ball to Tony. The plan was that Todd would run forward and Tony would pass it back to him. He would then shoot - a quick goal before the other team had got themselves organised!

It didn't work out that way. Tony collected the ball and passed it back, but Charlie Burnet intercepted the pass. Meanwhile another United player was moving up. Charlie crossed the ball to him. Tony tried to tackle, but the player sidestepped and shot at the goal.

Luckily Becky was ready. She made a
great save, booting the ball back up the
pitch to Mick. Mick tried to pass
forward to Todd. He got into a muddle
with his legs and lost the ball to a
United player.

The ball was soon back with Charlie.
This time he didn't pass. Bang! He shot
for goal. Becky dived desperately but
the ball was in the net.

By half time it was clear that the All-Stars were going to lose.

United had already scored six goals, and the All-Stars hadn't even had a decent shot at goal.

At last they got a chance. It was all down to Becky. She booted the ball brilliantly, right to Todd's feet. The United goalie was off his mark. Todd hammered the ball home!

Chapter 6 - You're the Problem

When Captain Robins blew the final whistle the score was 9 - 1 to the crew.

Todd and his team put a brave face on it. They thanked the captain and the crew, and said how much they had enjoyed it. If only the game hadn't been shown over the whole ship!

Charlie Burnet was chatting to the captain. He called Todd back.

"I'm really impressed with how well you organised your team. You didn't give up even though you were losing."

"Thanks," said Todd. "But we weren't very good, were we?"

Captain Robins laughed. "You can't expect to be yet. You know all about football, but you've never actually played before! You did very well for a first game, especially your goalie!

"But I think Mr Burnet has something else to say."

"That's right," said Charlie. "Now, do you know the main problem with your team?"

Todd shook his head.

"It's you! You've taken on too much. You're trying to be the captain and the coach. Now, what about taking on a new coach?"

"Who?"

"Me!"

Chapter 7 -
Captain Robins to the Rescue

The whole gang were thrilled that
Charlie was going to help them. There
were six weeks before the starship
reached the next planet, so Captain
Robins let them use the big hold for
training.

Some of the other youngsters on the
ship got interested, and they came
along too. None of the new players
were as good as the original All-Stars.

Charlie was a good coach. He managed
to sharpen up their skills, and gave
them confidence in their tackling.

"If only there was another team of our own age we could play," Todd said to Charlie.

"We could challenge the crew to a re-match, but I'm sure they would knock us flat again."

"I'm not so sure about that," said Charlie.

"But finding another team your age is a problem. There can't be one nearer than twenty light years!"

The rest of the team agreed. Then, once again, Captain Robins came to the rescue.

Chapter 8 - A Fixture

A message arrived for Todd at school
one day.

REPORT TO THE BRIDGE,
16,00 HOURS TODAY.

J Robins, Captain

Everyone in the school thought this was
great. They didn't get invited to the
bridge by the captain!

Todd hadn't been there very often.
It was an amazing place, full of
equipment to drive the Searcher
through twisting wormholes in space.
This was the only way the ship could
travel between the stars.

A man's face was on a screen on the captain's desk.

"This is Mr Hussein" said the captain. "He's on Astria. That's the planet we're heading for. I believe you play five-a-side football on Astria, Mr Hussein?"

"That's right," said Mr Hussein, "but we're not very experienced yet."

"Nor are we!" said the captain. "Here's Todd, captain of our under-15 team. Can you give him a game?"
"We'd be glad to!"

A week later, Searcher was in orbit over Astria. It was an ocean planet, with thousands of small islands where the people lived.

Soon the team were heading down in a shuttle craft. The crew's team were landing as well.

"Coming to support us?"

"No chance! We've got a game of our own. We've been challenged now!"

The Astria team came to meet the All Stars. They were very excited to be playing a team from a starship!

Chapter 9 - Winners and Losers!

The whistle blew. Todd back passed to Mick. The Astria team expected him to pass back to Todd and a player moved to intercept, but the All-Stars were ready with a trick Charlie had showed them. Mick tapped the ball sideways to Tim, who booted it up to a waiting Todd.

Bang! Todd shot, but hit the cross-bar.

That was close! The Astria players woke up. This starship team were good!

Astria had the ball now, and Becky had to make one of her brilliant saves.

But she was up for it, and the ball was soon moving the other way. Tony trapped it brilliantly, and passed it to Mick. Mick was well placed. With a flick it was in the back of the net. Goal!

The All-Stars were two up by half time. At the beginning of the second half, Astria pulled one back. They were playing much better now.

Then Tim made a mistake in defence and let a ball through. An Astria player pounced on it and fired at the goal.

Becky knew nothing about it until the ball was in the back of the net!

Two all. Two minutes to go. Todd took the ball on the left wing.

An Astria player came flying in for the tackle, but Todd used another of Charlie's tricks to dodge him.

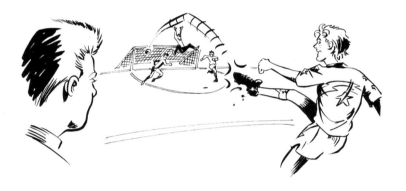

All the Astria players were falling back now. Their keeper couldn't see the ball. Todd lofted the ball over their heads. The keeper leapt - and missed! Three two! The All-Stars had won!

Later, on the shuttle home, Todd's team saw that the crew weren't celebrating.

"Come on," said Becky. "Tell us how you did."

"We lost seven - nil," said Charlie.

"And that's not the worst of it. They'd got cameras set up. Everyone on the planet was watching!"